My Grandmother's Stories

P9-CDT-643

My Grandmother's Stories

A COLLECTION OF JEWISH FOLK TALES

by Adèle Geras · illustrated by Jael Jordan

ALFRED A. KNOPF · NEW YORK

j 398.2
(1) MY

OLD HALL GREEN LIBRARY

This book is dedicated to the memory of
Pessia Mann Hamburger
(1880–1970)
A.G.

and for my family, my friends and Max
J.J.

────────────

I would like to thank Alan Untermann, Dorothy Collins and
especially my mother, Leah Weston, for their advice and help.
A.G.

────────────

Two books were very helpful to me while I was writing these
stories. They are:

The Complete Family Guide to Jewish Holidays
by Dalia Hardof Renberg (Robson Books, 1987)

A Treasury of Jewish Folklore
edited by Nathan Ausubel (Valentine Mitchell, 1972)

────────────

THIS IS A BORZOI BOOK PUBLISHED BY ALFRED A. KNOPF, INC.

Text copyright © 1990 by Adèle Geras
Illustrations copyright © 1990 by Jael Jordan
All rights reserved under International and Pan-American Copyright Conventions.
Published in the United States by Alfred A. Knopf, Inc., New York. Distributed by
Random House, Inc., New York. Published in Great Britain by
Heinemann Young Books, London.

Manufactured in Hong Kong 1 2 3 4 5 6 7 8 9 10

Library of Congress Cataloging-in-Publication Data
Geras, Adèle. My grandmother's stories/by Adèle Geras; illustrated by
Jael Jordan   p.   cm.
Contents: Bavsi's feast – The faces of the czar – The golden shoes – The tablecloth – A
tangle of wools – Saving the pennies – The garden of talking flowers – The market of
miseries – An overcrowded house – A phantom at the wedding
ISBN 0-679-80910-4 ISBN 0-679-90910-9 (lib. bdg.)
1. Children's stories, American [1. Soviet Union – Fiction. 2. Short stories.] I. Jordan,
Jael, ill. II. Title. – PZ7. G29354My 1990 [Fic] – dc20 90–4309 CIP   AC

CONTENTS

Bavsi's Feast

FIRST of all, let me tell you about my grandmother's kitchen. It was a small, square room with a large sink next to one wall, and a wooden table pushed up to another. Because my

grandmother lived on the third floor of an apartment house, the window in one wall was really a door and opened out onto a small balcony. In summer there would be tall, glass jars lined up on a table on the balcony; and in the jars tiny, green cucumbers floated in a pale, cloudy liquid, turning into pickles in the sunlight. If only you could taste the dishes that my grandmother cooked: cinnamon cakes, braided loaves of bread, meats stewed in velvety sauces, fish fried to the color of gold, soup with matzo dumplings, fragrant with nutmeg; and for the Sabbath, the kugel: a pudding made of noodles and eggs, with just a hint of burnt sugar to give it its caramel color and smoky taste. One of the tasks I enjoyed was helping to mince things. I liked using a carrot to poke whatever we were mincing deep into the silver mouth of the machine clamped to the side of the table. My grandmother liked chopping and talking.

One day, we were making a strudel, cutting up apples to mix with the nuts and raisins.

"Have you ever thought," she said to me, "what it must be like to be hungry?"

"I'm often hungry," I answered. "I'm hungry now. May I eat the rest of this apple?"

My grandmother laughed. "That's not hunger. That's greed. Let me tell you a story about someone who learned what real hunger meant. He was a merchant, a very rich merchant, who lived a long time ago, in the days of King Solomon."

"Where did he live?"

"He lived in Jerusalem. And he was the stingiest, most penny-pinching scoundrel who ever drew breath. He was so stingy that he never even married, not wishing to have the additional expense of a wife and children. All over the city people talked of his stinginess. His name became famous. 'Stingy as Bavsi,' people would say, or sometimes 'evil as Bavsi.' Now, one day, a great famine came to the land. The crops had failed and the poor people began to suffer from lack of food. Rich men who were also kind distributed all the contents of their granaries among the starving citizens, but not Bavsi, oh no. Do you know what he did?"

"What?"

"He put huge wooden bars across the doors of his granaries to keep the people out. He cut down on his servants' food and sold his grain at a very high price to those who could manage to scrape together the money. So he grew rich while others starved and suffered. All the stories whispered by those who had good reason to hate him at last reached the ears of King Solomon himself, and when he learned how Bavsi was behaving, he decided to teach the miser a lesson he would not forget."

"What did he do?"

"He sent the Royal Chamberlain to Bavsi's house with an invitation. The merchant was to take dinner with the King the very next evening. You can imagine how overwhelmed, how excited, and how flattered Bavsi was. 'At last!' he said to himself, 'King Solomon realizes what a great man I am. How rich! How powerful!' He called his servants at once and set them to work, washing his clothes and setting out his jewels ready for dinner the next day.

When he woke up in the morning, Bavsi decided not to eat at

all that day. King Solomon's feast was sure to be sumptuous beyond dreams. It would be a pity, therefore, not to do it full justice. So at six o'clock, Bavsi presented himself at King Solomon's palace. The sun was just setting, and the palace walls were pearly in the apricot light of evening. Bavsi's servants had carried him through the streets on a raised platform, so that the hem of his robe would not become dusty. On every side there were men dressed in rags and lean with hunger; children who no longer had any energy left for playing; and women with sunken eyes that were red from weeping. Bavsi saw none of them. He fixed his eyes on Solomon's glittering walls and his mind on the feast that was waiting for him. The truth of the matter was that he was already extremely hungry, not having eaten since the previous night.

In the palace, Bavsi followed the servant who waited at the door to where the Royal Chamberlain was seated, in a wide hall hung with embroideries in the colors of every jewel dug from the earth or found in the depths of the sea.

'Ah, Bavsi,' said the Royal Chamberlain. 'Approach and let me make you welcome! Let me also explain to you how you must behave while you are a guest in the palace. There is, as I'm sure you'll understand, a very rigid form of etiquette on these occasions: certain rules that have to be obeyed.'

'Of course, of course,' said Bavsi, nodding eagerly. 'I understand perfectly.'

'Very well, then,' said the Royal Chamberlain. 'First of all, you must never, at any time, ask for anything: not from the King, nor from his servants, nor from anyone else. Agreed?'

'Agreed,' said Bavsi. 'What could I possibly need to ask for?' He chuckled happily.

'Secondly,' the Royal Chamberlain continued, 'whatever you may see happening, you must not ask any questions or utter any complaints.'

'Questions?' said Bavsi. 'Complaints? From me? Never in a million years!'

'And lastly,' said the Royal Chamberlain, 'when King Solomon asks you whether you are enjoying your meal, you must be as lavish as you can be in praising it. Is that understood?'

'It will be my pleasure,' Bavsi said with a smile. 'My pleasure entirely.'

'Thank you,' said the Royal Chamberlain. 'I do not have to remind you how terrible the King's anger will be if you do not obey these three rules. Now, if you will follow me, dinner is still being prepared. It will be ready in one hour. You are the only guest at this feast. I will ask you to wait here, until the King is ready to dine.'

Bavsi was shown into a small room that looked out onto the courtyard. By now, he was beginning to feel quite faint from hunger, and the very worst thing of all was that there was no door to this small room, and the palace kitchens were just across the courtyard. Every wonderful smell in the world rose up out of that kitchen and drifted through the evening air, straight to where Bavsi was sitting: fragrances that tormented him more than if they had been ghosts from another world."

"What sort of smells?" I asked my grandmother.

"Everything you can think of that's wonderful: bread baking

to a golden crust, onions frying, cinnamon lingering in the air, meat roasting in aromatic oils, spices being pounded in stone jars, rose petals being steeped in water, ready to be crystallized in sugar — every good smell that there could be in a kitchen was there that night. I can almost find it in my heart to feel sorry for Bavsi, but not quite. He was only a little sorry for himself, for he comforted himself with the thought that soon, very soon, he would be eating alone with the great King and conversing with the wisest man in all the world. It was worth waiting for.

At last, the moment arrived and Bavsi was led into the room in which King Solomon was waiting for him, lying on cushions made of silk and embroidered with threads of silver.

'Sit, Bavsi,' said King Solomon, 'and let us eat.' Bavsi sat, and a servant carried in a bowl of soup like liquid gold and set it before King Solomon. Another servant followed with a bowl, which he set in front of Bavsi, but before the merchant could pick up his spoon, a third servant took Bavsi's bowl and carried it away, leaving the unfortunate creature holding his spoon up in the air. He was just about to say something when he remembered his promise to the Royal Chamberlain, so he smiled at the King while the devils of hunger began to move around in his stomach, so that he felt pain and nausea and dizziness as he watched Solomon smacking his lips with every mouthful.

After the soup came a whole fish baked in vine leaves and laid on a bed of rice. Then came roasted meats. Then cakes dripping with honey and studded with nuts, and velvety fruits fragrant with luscious juices, and with each course the same thing

happened: the food was taken away from Bavsi before he had time to touch it. Bavsi felt completely bewildered.

'How are you enjoying your meal?' King Solomon asked.

And Bavsi, remembering his promise, said, 'It is the most wondrous meal I have ever eaten.' Meanwhile, he was thinking: Not long now. Soon this torment will be over. I will leave the palace and return to my own house and eat my food. It may be plain, but it is food. Soon, soon I will be gone from here.

But Bavsi had reckoned without King Solomon.

'Stay and listen to some music,' the King said, and Bavsi had to stay, for the ruler's word was law. When the musicians had left, and Bavsi rose to go, King Solomon said, 'You must stay the night. It is far too late for you to go home. The servants will show you to your bedchamber.'

Bavsi did not sleep at all. His hunger was gnawing at him, just as though a large rat had taken up residence in his stomach, and it was not only hunger that was troubling him.

'Why,' he said to himself, 'has the King done this to me? He has deliberately kept all food and drink from me. It must be a punishment. He must be teaching me something. What have I learned? Only the meaning of real hunger, so that must be what King Solomon intended.'

When Bavsi arrived at his own house the next morning, he threw open his granary doors and distributed his corn to the poor, and never again sold food to the starving people to make a profit for himself. There. Now you can have a piece of apple."

THE FACES OF THE CZAR

THE cupboard in my grandmother's bedroom was big and brown, with a long mirror set into its central panel. If you opened the cupboard doors, there were shelves upon shelves filled with sheets and pillowcases, towels and tablecloths, and even some containing folded underwear and lots of rolled-up brown balls of stockings. Right at the bottom there was a

drawer, and it was in this drawer that the button box was kept. It was made of tin: a dull, silvery color. I don't know what used to be kept in it, or what it had held when it first came into the house; but now it was full of buttons. When I took it out of the drawer and moved it around in my hands, all the buttons made a sushy-rattly sound as they moved against the metal sides of the box. I liked spilling them onto the black and yellow tiles of the bedroom floor, where I arranged them in groups according to size, or color, or beauty, or spread them out in huge patterns all around me. Sometimes, my cousins and I used the buttons as pretend money. Silver ones were the most valuable of all, and there were six buttons (from a dress that had once belonged to my aunt in America) that had the face of a man with a beard and a crown scratched onto them.

"Such a face," my grandmother said, "could only belong to a Czar. Do you know what a Czar was?"

I shook my head.

"A Czar was a Russian emperor, the kind of ruler whose very lightest word was law, the kind of ruler before whom everyone trembled, and more especially the poor peasant, trying to scratch a bare living out of a tiny patch of ground. And of course, as well as being powerful, and wicked more often than not, Czars, like all other rulers, were in the habit of having little pictures of themselves stamped onto every coin in the kingdom. All this talk of Czars reminds me of the story of Frankel the farmer. Have I told you about him before?"

"No, never," I said. "Tell me about him now."

"So put all the buttons back in the box and I'll begin.

"Are they all in? Good. Now, long ago, in a very faraway and neglected corner of Russia, about a day's ride from the Czar's Summer Palace, there lived a farmer called Frankel. On this particular day that I'm telling you of, Frankel was happily occupied digging up turnips in what he called his field, but which in truth was a piece of land about the size of a tablecloth. He was content. The sun was shining for once, the turnips had all turned out well, large and pleasantly mauve and white in color, and their leaves were so prettily green and feathery that Frankel sang as he worked. He was absorbed in his labors, so that he hardly noticed the horseman drawing nearer and nearer, until the noise of the hoofbeats on the dry earth of the road made him look up. What he saw made him drop his spade in amazement. It was the Czar. Frankel bowed deeply.

'Do not be surprised, my friend,' said the Czar. 'Often, when I'm sick to death of court councils and endless feasts, I saddle my horse and go riding about my kingdom, talking to my subjects. I am very interested to observe that although the hair on your head is gray, the hairs of your beard are still black. It's something I've often noticed in people before, and yet no one seems to know the reason for it.'

'O mighty Czar,' Frankel replied (reasoning that he couldn't possibly be too polite to a Czar), 'I am only a poor Jewish farmer, but the reason is this. The hairs on my head started growing when I was born. Those on my chin only started growing when I was thirteen years old, after the bar mitzvah ceremony at which I became a man. Therefore, the hairs on my chin are much younger and not yet gray.'

'Amazing!' said the Czar. 'How simple and yet how logical! I'm overjoyed to have discovered the answer to a question that has long been puzzling me. Now, I beg of you, my friend, tell no one else what you have told me. Let it remain a secret between us. Do you agree?'

'I will only reveal our secret after I have seen your face a hundred times, sire,' said Frankel. So the Czar set off on his horse, chuckling to himself, and Frankel continued digging up his turnips.

When the Czar arrived at the palace, he asked all his advisers to gather around.

'Here,' he said, 'is a question. Why does the hair on the head grow gray before the hair of the beard? Whoever can answer that question for me will be promoted to the position of Chief Adviser to the Czar, and will sit in a specially fashioned silver throne studded with lumps of amber the size of small onions.'

All the advisers scurried about, asking everyone they met, consulting books too heavy to be carried, and working out every possibility on scrolls of paper a yard long. This went on for weeks. Finally, two of the chancellors discussed the matter.

'I remember,' said one, 'that on the day the Czar asked us the question, he had come back from a ride to the Western Territory. Perhaps he found the answer there. If we ride in the same direction, maybe we'll come across it too.'

Thus it happened that one rainy day as Frankel was listening sadly to the sucking noises made by his boots entering and leaving the mud, two horsemen galloped up to where he was standing.

'Good day to you, farmer,' said one of the horsemen. 'We are advisers to the Czar, and we have reason to think that the Czar may have ridden this way a few weeks ago.'

'He did,' Frankel agreed. 'And now, here you are. This part of the world hasn't ever been quite so busy. A person hardly has the leisure to tend his property.'

'But did you tell the Czar why it is that the hair on the head turns gray before the hair of the beard?'

'I did, but I'm not at liberty to tell you gentlemen.'

The chancellors sighed. 'Is there nothing we can do to persuade you to change your mind?'

Frankel considered. 'One hundred silver rubles will change my mind instantly.'

'Then take these, my friend,' said one of the chancellors, 'and tell us the answer to the riddle.'

Frankel took the coins, sat down in the road, and spread the coins out on his lap to count them. When he had finished, he told the Czar's advisers exactly what he had told the Czar. The men sprang into their saddles and left for the palace at a gallop, feeling very pleased with themselves, but not as pleased as Frankel, who had suddenly acquired wealth.

The trouble only began when they came to the Czar and told him the answer.

'How can you possibly know this?' shouted the Czar.

'We met a Jewish farmer called Frankel on the road,' they said, 'and he told us.'

'And he undertook to say nothing, the scoundrel!' The Czar stamped his foot and sent for his Chief of Police. 'Go to the farm of the Jew, Frankel, and bring him here at once. Also, alert the firing squad. This will be Frankel's last day on earth.'

Well, eventually the Police brought Frankel to see the Czar.

'What have you to say for yourself, you wretch?' yelled the Czar. 'Did you not promise me that you would not reveal the secret you told me?'

'I said,' Frankel whispered, 'that I would only reveal it after I had seen your face a hundred times.'

'But this is only the second time you have seen me, you worm! What have you to say for yourself before I have you shot?'

'Forgive me, Czar,' said Frankel, and he took out the bag containing the hundred silver rubles which the chancellors had given him. 'Here are one hundred coins. I have looked at every one. Therefore, I'm sure you will agree, I have seen your face one hundred times.'

The Czar was stunned, full of admiration for Frankel's sharp wits.

'I shall get rid of all my advisers and appoint you instead,' he chuckled. 'You shall sit at my left hand on a silver throne studded with amber lumps the size of small onions. You shall want for nothing, my friend.'

And so Frankel lived to a ripe old age, and became the richest and most powerful man in Russia, next only to the Czar himself.''

THE GOLDEN SHOES

THERE were other cupboards in my grandmother's apartment, as well as the big brown one in her bedroom. In the room where only the grandest of guests were entertained, there was a long, blue sofa and next to it, a glass-fronted cabinet full of books. I was allowed to turn the brass key and open the doors, and take out some of the books.

"The ones on the top shelf are too heavy for you," my grand-mother used to say, and I never minded because they looked dark and stiff in their leather covers, and the pages crackled as they turned, as though they might break if you touched them. I used to take out the smaller books on the lower shelves, and sniff the pages. I knew the little black marks on the paper were words because sometimes my grandmother would read a story aloud to me, but mainly I liked the smell. Every book has a special fragrance: a mixture of ink and glue and a distant memory of the trees that the paper was made from, but I've never found other books that smelled as good as those that lived behind glass in the cabinet next to the long sofa.

In the dining room, a sideboard took up most of one wall. On top of the sideboard lived two brass bowls filled with fruit. Under the bowls there were round lace mats that my aunt Sara had crocheted from silky threads. At the bottom of the sideboard, there were three sets of wooden doors for me to open. One cupboard I closed immediately: there was nothing in it but glasses—wineglasses with twisted stems, plain water-glasses, tiny little glasses that no one ever used, and a brand-new set of tumblers, which had pictures of red flowers painted all around the tops. My aunts, Miriam and Dina, had sent them all the way from America.

The next cupboard held the silver box full of spices, which my grandmother used to let me sniff at, every Saturday evening as she said the prayers for the beginning of another week. There were pictures and patterns on every side of the box, cut into the silver so that you could go over the long, curly beards of the men with your fingertips, or follow the outlines of the birds and animals. Also in this cupboard lived the candlesticks (brass ones for every day and silver ones for special occasions), the embroidered cloths for covering up the braided loaves of Sabbath bread, a few spare velvet skull caps (in case visitors forgot to bring theirs when they came to a Sabbath dinner), and some square prayerbooks that had pages rimmed with gold paint.

The last cupboard of all was the best. In it, my grandmother kept boxes of crystallized fruit, Turkish delight, and chocolate. She wrapped the boxes up in newspaper, very carefully, but I knew what was hidden and so did my cousins. We'd open the door and put our noses in, and breathe the velvety chocolate smell, but no one ever dared to steal from this cupboard because my grandmother always knew exactly what she'd wrapped up, and how much of everything was left over after she'd distributed the day's treat. This always happened after dinner.

"Go to the cupboard," she'd say to me, "and bring me the flat parcel next to the wall." Or "Bring me the little parcel on the right-hand side at the back," and I would bring it, and wait to see what would be unwrapped. The grownups would drink their lemon tea (from the American glasses, which fitted into little plastic holders, so that you could pick them up without burning yourself), and we would eat flat rectangles of chocolate on which a word had been stamped in lovely, curly letters. My grandmother read it out to me.

"That says 'Splendide.'" She nodded wisely. "It's the French word for splendid." I thought that the word described the chocolate very well.

The best cupboard of all was in the bedroom and it wasn't really a cupboard at all, just a small set of shelves with a curtain hanging on a wire that you could pull across to hide the rows and rows of shoes that were kept there. Most of the shoes belonged to my aunt Sara.

"She has such small feet," my grandmother used to say to me. "Not much bigger than yours. And how she loves to buy shoes!"

Whenever I looked on the shelves, all the buckles and pointed toes and dainty heels, all the different colors of the leather — brown and black and white and pink — seemed to say to me, try us on . . . don't be afraid. I used to pick out a pair I thought looked pretty, and put my bare feet into them. Then I would walk up and down, making sure to stay in front of the mirror so that I could see myself being a lady. The hard little heels rang on the black and yellow tiles, and up and down I went, glancing over my shoulder as I walked away from the mirror to see if I looked more like a lady from the back than from the front.

"You remind me," my grandmother said to me one day when I had chosen to put on a pair of silver sandals, "of the story of the Wisest Man in Chelm."

"Where's Chelm?" I said. "And who was the wisest man? And why do I remind you of him?"

"Take the silver sandals off and put them away and I'll tell you."

I put the sandals back on the shelf, pulled the curtain carefully across, hiding the beautiful shoes, and went to sit beside my grandmother on the bed.

"Chelm," she said, "is a small town which, they say, is right in the middle of Poland. Or perhaps it's Hungary. Because it isn't a real place, because you can't find it on any map, and that means you can put it anywhere you like."

I smiled. "It's a magic place. It's somewhere you've made up."

"Me? I couldn't make up such a place if I live to be a hundred and twenty," said my grandmother. "Always, for as long as I can remember, there have been stories told about the people of Chelm, and believe me, there's nothing magic about them. On the contrary, every single person who ever lived in the town of Chelm was a fool."

"Not one clever person in the whole town?" I asked.

"Not one. Fools, dolts, idiots, and simpletons, from the teacher to the butcher, from the carpenter to the baker. And not only them, their wives and children too. They were fools as well."

"Were they happy?"

"They were as happy and as unhappy as anyone else, I suppose, but they had their own ways of solving problems."

"Did they have a problem about shoes?"

"Not about shoes, not exactly. What happened, happened like this. One day, all the people of Chelm decided that there should be a Council of Wise Men to look after the day-to-day business of the town. Ten people were chosen to be the Council, and then those ten people chose the cleverest among them to be the Chief Sage."

"But were they really clever?" I asked.

"No, they were fools. Everyone in Chelm is a fool, whether his name is Chief Sage or not. You must remember that."

"I will. What happened next?"

"The Council of Wise Men decided that the Chief Sage should wear a special pair of golden shoes whenever he walked about the town, so that everyone would recognize him and see that he *was* the Chief Sage and not just an ordinary citizen. The shoemaker made a beautiful pair of sparkling golden shoes, and the Chief Sage put them on at once and went walking about the town. Unfortunately, it had been raining the night before and the streets were deep in mud. The Chief Sage had hardly taken twenty steps before his beautiful shoes were covered in mud and not the tiniest speck of gold could be seen. 'This will never do,' he said to the Council of Wise Men. 'No one could see my gold shoes because of the mud. What is the solution to the problem?' The Council of Wise Men sat up all night debating the matter, and by morning they had found the answer: the shoemaker would make a pair of ordinary brown boots, which the Chief Sage could slip on over his golden shoes, thus keeping the mud away from their glittering surface. Oh, the Council of Wise Men was delighted with this solution, and so was the Chief Sage, and he stepped out happily in his golden shoes with the brown leather boots on over the top. To his amazement, however, not one single citizen of Chelm recognized him while he was walking through the town.

'No one recognized me!' he cried to the Council of Wise Men. 'They couldn't see the golden shoes because of the brown boots covering them up!'

'Aah!' sighed the Council of Wise Men. 'How clever of you to have worked that out! It's not for nothing we elected you to be our Chief Sage!' They sighed again. 'But what is to be done?'

One of the Council had a moment of inspiration. 'I know!' he cried. 'Let the shoemaker cut a pattern of small holes along the side of the brown boots, and right across the toes, and then the golden shoes will be visible through the holes!'

Murmurs of 'Brilliant!' and 'Wonderful!' rippled round the Council Chamber. The brown boots were taken to the shoemaker, and he punched a pattern of small, star-shaped holes all over the leather. The Chief Sage put them on as soon as they were ready, and set off for another walk around the town . . . but again the streets were muddy, and the mud came through the holes and hid the golden shoes.

No one recognized the Chief Sage and everyone in the Council of Wise Men was in despair. They discussed the problem for many days and many nights, and at last arrived at a perfect solution. Now, if you go to Chelm and walk around, you will know at once who the wisest man in the whole town is. It's quite clear. He's the one who walks about with a pair of golden shoes on his hands, wearing them as though they were gloves!"

I laughed and said, "Tell me another story about Chelm. Are there any more stories?"

"There are many," said my grandmother. "I'll tell you another one another day."

"No, now. Please now. Just a very little story."

"Like the one about the bread and butter?"

"Is that a little story?"

"It's a very small story indeed."

"Then tell it."

"Very well," said my grandmother. "Two men of science in Chelm were discussing a very interesting question. When you drop a piece of bread and butter on the floor, does it always fall with the buttery side down?

Yankel said, 'Yes, it always does.'

Mandel said, 'No, it only falls like that sometimes.'

'I will prove it to you,' Yankel said. 'I will butter a slice of bread and drop it on the floor, and you will see what you will see!'

He buttered a slice of bread and dropped it on the floor. It fell with the dry side down and the buttery side up.

'You see,' said Mandel triumphantly, 'I was right. It fell with the buttery side up.'

'Nonsense,' said Yankel. 'It was my fault. I made a mistake. I buttered the wrong side, that's all!' "

THE TABLECLOTH

OUTSIDE the front door of my grandmother's apartment there was a flight of stairs leading to the roof: a wide, flat area bordered by a stone parapet where all the families in the building used to hang their washing. If you went up on laundry day, the whole roof was a-flutter with damp sheets and table-cloths, flapping shirts and blouses, scarves like flags waving, flocks of white handkerchiefs like doves, and here and there, strange and wonderful garments which made my cousins and me laugh behind my grandmother's back: Mrs. Sirkis's huge lace-edged bloomers, and the long, skinny, striped socks belonging to the dentist who lived on the first floor. The clothes on the washing line smelled strongly of pale yellow soap, and were held on the line by wooden clothes pins that had been bleached pale gray by the sun. My grandmother used to bring the wet clothes up to the roof in a big tin tub. This tub had a handle on each side, and once the clothes were hung up, it was light enough for me to hold on to one of the handles and help my grandmother carry it downstairs again.

The roof seemed very high up to me. There were days when it frightened me to look over the parapet and down, down, down into the street. Far below us, I could see the door to Genzel's shop, and although the things that people were buying were in their baskets as they came out, my grandmother knew exactly what everyone had gone to the shop for.

"There's Mrs. Rakov buying herrings," she'd say. "She is making chopped herring tonight. And look, there's Mr. Lapidas, a dozen bagels and cream cheese, that's what he likes

31

for his lunch, bagels and cheese. Mrs. Blumberg needs onions . . . there were none in her kitchen yesterday, this I saw with my own eyes." And so on.

I liked going to Genzel's shop. It was so near the apartment that sometimes my grandmother would put money in my hand and send me down there for something: a few ounces of cheese or a package of tea. I followed the stairs, around and around and around from the third floor to the street, quite by myself, and then I carefully crossed over the little side road and went into the dark treasure cave of Genzel's shop. I wasn't frightened because I knew that my grandmother was watching me from the balcony, and I always waved at her from the corner.

Genzel's shelves were filled with tins and boxes, and the small room smelled of soap and salt and cheese and wax, the silver herrings in the big, brown barrel, the shiny black olives floating in inky water, and the round yellow cheeses on the counter. Sacks of flour stood open by the entrance, and there was candy in glass jars near the drawer where Mrs. Genzel kept her money. Strings of onions hung from the ceiling, and tall people went into the shop with their heads bent. Genzel was thin and wore a dusty black jacket. Mrs. Genzel was fat and if you didn't watch out, she'd pinch your cheek between her thumb and forefinger, muttering endearments, or even give you a fishy-smelling kiss. I used to ask for whatever I wanted and Genzel would get it for me, wrap it in newspaper and put it in my basket, and take my money and give me change. Mrs. Genzel would give me a wonderful candy like a marble that tasted of aniseed and changed color as I sucked it.

My cousin Danny and I had a special game that we used to play on the roof. We'd collected lots of broken clothes pins and hidden the tiny pieces of wood under a bucket. We used to wait until a man wearing a hat went past, far, far below us in the street, and then we'd throw a piece of clothes pin over the parapet and lean over to see whether it had landed in the man's hat, or at least near enough to make him look up. If anyone *did* look up, we used to crouch down where we couldn't be seen and laugh and laugh.

One day in spring, as I was looking over the edge, waiting for my grandmother to finish hanging out the washing, I saw something astonishing.

"Come quickly and look," I said to my grandmother. "There's a man walking past with an animal curled round his head . . . it must be asleep."

My grandmother looked. "Silly girl! Haven't you seen a streimel before?"

"What's a streimel?"

"A hat with fur all around the crown."

"Oh. Well, maybe I have seen one, but it looks different from up here. Not like a fur hat at all. Just like a cat wrapped around the man's head. Why is he wearing a fur hat on such a warm day?"

"Because it's a kind of uniform. It shows that that man is very religious. He spends most of his days studying the Scriptures. His mind, you see, is on higher things than hats, or whether he's feeling too warm. He may even," said my grandmother, "be a rabbi. You know what a rabbi is, don't you?"

"Oh, yes," I said. "He leads services in the synagogue."

"And that's not all he does," said my grandmother. "Rabbis have to be especially clever men, not only because they are dealing with God's work all day long, but also because they have to give advice, settle arguments, help everyone to live together peacefully. It's a difficult job, I can tell you. Just like being in charge of an enormous family. Of course, the cleverest rabbi I ever knew was Rabbi Samuels, who lived down there." She pointed to a spot near the horizon, and I craned my head to see, fully expecting Rabbi Samuels to be visible, perhaps even to be waving at us. "He's dead now, poor man," my grandmother continued, "but he was the cleverest rabbi who ever lived, and do you know why?"

"Why?"

"Because he married a clever woman. Her name was Rivka, and while he studied the holy texts and communicated with the Almighty, she looked and listened and went to the shop and the market and talked to everyone and knew everything, which meant that she could give the Rabbi excellent advice from time to time. Oh, the Rabbi acquired such a reputation for cleverness, thanks to her, people came from miles around to ask him about their problems . . . as they did in the matter of the tablecloth."

"Tell me the story of the tablecloth," I said.

My grandmother sat down on the upturned tin tub, and began.

"Long ago, when I was a little girl, there were no modern buildings like this one, with apartments one on top of another. No, the people lived in rooms around four sides of a courtyard.

In our courtyard, we used to sit outside in summer on chairs taken from the dining room. There were big flowerpots with geraniums growing in them, and sometimes a family would put a rabbit hutch in the courtyard and all the children would come and try to stroke the rabbit through the wire. The courtyard was also the place where washing was hung out to dry.

On one side of the building lived a woman called Pnina with her family; and on the other side, directly opposite, lived a women called Malka with her husband and children. Now Pnina's name means 'pearl,' and truly, she was a pearl among women: kind and thoughtful and loving and friendly. Malka's name means 'queen,' and that is what she felt she should have been. But of course, she was not a queen, so her whole life was spoiled by envying others their good fortune, and by moaning constantly about her dreadful luck. No one liked her. Even her own family found her tiring and annoying, which naturally gave her even more to complain about. And so life went on for some time.

Now Malka thought everyone better off than herself, but Pnina aroused in her feelings of desperate envy. On Thursdays, when Pnina hung out her newly washed tablecloth, ready for the Sabbath, Malka's heart folded itself into little pleats of anguish, for the tablecloth was something out of a dream, and it was Pnina's and not hers."

"What was it like?" I wanted to know.

"Oh, huge and white and shining. When the wind sprang up behind it and made it billow out over the courtyard, it was as though a beautiful white swan had spread its wings, or as though a tall ship had sailed into the courtyard. All over the white linen there were damasked patterns of whiter lilies and roses that caught the light and glowed like satin. Round the sides there were tiny squares of drawn threadwork, and the cloth was edged with finest lace. Oh, it was something to see. Now, let me continue with the story. Everyone knew that the cloth had been sent to Pnina when she was married, by a rich uncle who lived in Warsaw. We all knew the tablecloth well. That's what made Malka's behavior all the more astonishing."

"Tell me."

"I'm telling you. One day, Pnina must have been in a hurry to hang out the washing, because when the wind started to blow, it lifted the clothes pins off the line and sent the tablecloth flying right over to the far side of the courtyard, where it landed outside Malka's kitchen door. Now, Malka had been filling partly cooked cabbage leaves with spoonfuls of rice and fried onions and carrots and little pieces of meat, and rolling them up into neat, pale-green parcels, and putting them into the pot, ready to cover with water and lemon juice. They had to cook slowly, slowly, for the evening meal. When she glanced out of the window and saw the tablecloth, she did not hesitate for a moment. She washed her hands, and stepping out into the courtyard, she picked up the tablecloth, shook it out in full view of everyone, and began to fold it. It was then that Pnina noticed what had happened. She came running across to where Malka was standing.

'Oh, Malka,' she said, 'thank you for catching my tablecloth.

The wind must have blown it over here . . . and thank you for folding it so well.'

Malka gave a sugary smile. 'I'm afraid you're mistaken. This is *my* tablecloth. It does look rather like the one you show off to us every day almost, but alas, this cloth is mine.'

'No.' Pnina went white. 'It's mine. It was a wedding present from my uncle in Warsaw. I know it as well as I know my own children's faces.'

Malka laughed. 'You are not the only one with relations. I have an aunt in Cracow. She sent me the tablecloth. You are surely not saying that Cracow tablecloths are inferior to Warsaw tablecloths?'

'No, no . . .' Pnina was nearly weeping. 'I am only saying that that is *my* tablecloth.'

'And I am saying it's mine.'

'But it isn't . . .'

'It is.'

'It isn't.'

A crowd of neighbors gathered around the two women. Matters could have gone on like this for hours, but then someone shouted out, 'Go to Rabbi Samuels. Let him decide whose tablecloth it is.'

'A good idea,' said all the neighbors.

So Malka and Pnina set off for Rabbi Samuels's house, with Malka still clutching the tablecloth to her rather ample bosom.

The Rabbi sat in his chair, next to the table and listened to the two women telling their stories. The Rabbi's wife, Rivka, was in the kitchen, making chopped liver, mashing the meat up with chicken fat and an onion very finely chopped, and adding a little bit of parsley and salt and pepper. This task, however, did not prevent her from hearing every word that Pnina and Malka were saying. She always left the kitchen door open. Glancing at her husband in his chair, and observing the manner in which he was stroking his beard, Rivka realized that the Rabbi had no immediate solution to the problem.

'Beloved,' she called from the kitchen, 'would you be good enough to come here for one moment?'

'Excuse me, ladies,' said the Rabbi, glad of the opportunity to consult his wife. He left Pnina and Malka standing next to his chair, while he went into the kitchen, taking the tablecloth with him. Pnina and Malka leaned forward to hear what the Rabbi was saying to his wife, but at first they heard only whisperings. Then in Rivka's voice came these words, which Pnina and Malka both heard quite clearly.

'What a magnificent tablecloth! Such a pity about this tiny, tiny stain of red wine here in this corner.'

'Yes,' the Rabbi could be heard saying. 'A great shame indeed!'

When the Rabbi came out of the kitchen, he was smiling.

'Now, ladies, it has, luckily, been very easy for me to make a decision in this matter. Which of you has a tablecloth with a small pink wine stain in one corner?'

Malka's eyes sparkled. 'Oh, that's me! Four Sabbaths ago, my little boy, Eliezer, spilled the wine. Even though I put salt on it at once, a pink stain still remains. There is nothing I can do about it. It just won't come out.'

'And what have you to say to that, Pnina?' asked the Rabbi. 'Is she telling the truth?'

'Yes,' said Pnina, 'she must be, because of one thing I am quite certain: there were no wine stains on my tablecloth. My tablecloth is white all over.'

With a wide sweep of his arms like a fisherman casting a net over water, the Rabbi spread the cloth out for Pnina and Malka to see.

'This, then, must be Pnina's cloth,' he said, smiling, 'because as you can see, both of you, there is no stain of any kind anywhere upon it.'

Pnina took her property lovingly back into her arms, and thanked the Rabbi. Malka was disgraced, and although she was seething with rage at the Rabbi's trick, there was nothing at all she could say. Her stuffed cabbage had nearly boiled dry by the time she returned to her kitchen. 'Nothing ever goes right for me,' she sighed as she ate her food.

Pnina continued to serve her Sabbath dinner on the beautiful tablecloth till the day she died. And thanks to his wife's quick thinking, Rabbi Samuels became known throughout the neighborhood as the wisest of men."

A TANGLE OF WOOLS

I N the dining room of my grandmother's apartment, along with a large table, eight wooden chairs and the sideboard, there was a bed pushed up against one wall. This was only used as a bed at night. During the day it was covered with a dark cloth and became a divan for people to sit on. My grandmother put cushions on it, to make it look more comfortable. On the wall beside it hung two of the things I liked best in the world. First, and highest up the wall, so high that I couldn't touch it even if I stood on the bed, was a very large photograph of an aunt of mine who had died before I was born. This photograph showed a dark-haired lady in a lacy blouse with a very high collar. I liked her because she looked beautiful and gentle, and because I shared her name. There she was, every day, leaning on her hand and looking out at everyone from inside the square made by the heavy black wood of the frame around her portrait. Below this picture hung the Cross Stitch Mountains. No one else called them that. It was my name for them. Everyone else called them 'The Tapestry.' The Cross Stitch Mountains covered almost the whole wall behind the bed, and when I stood next to it, my head only came about halfway up the pattern. I never really knew who embroidered all the millions and millions of cross-stitches onto the canvas, in all those colors: red and yellow and orange and black and green. The stitches gathered themselves together into shapes like zigzagging peaks of mountains. First, there'd be a small line of pointed black triangles, then bigger green ones on top of them, then orange, then blue, then green again. All the way up the canvas: never-ending ranges of mountains piled up, one on top of another. I used to think that perhaps my dead aunt had made it and that was why it hung below her picture, but my grandmother told me once that all her daughters, even my mother, had taken their turn and added their own stitches to the pattern.

"You should have seen us," she would say to me, "in the days when your mother was a girl! There was wool all over this house. It reminds me of the story of the 'plonter.' "

"What's that? What's a 'plonter'?"

"A 'plonter' is a mess of tangled wools, all bundled up together in a basket."

"Is there a story about that?" I asked.

"Certainly," said my grandmother. "There is a story about almost everything. Now, let me see . . . where shall I begin? You know, don't you, that in the olden days . . . well, not really such olden days, because it happened to me . . . parents chose a suitable husband or wife for their child. They would look around at the children of other families whom they knew, and think: perhaps young Selig, or Ruth, will be a good husband, or wife, for our child. And then a matchmaker would run between the two families arranging meetings and seeing if the two young people were suitable for each other."

"What happened if you didn't like the person your parents chose for you?" I asked.

"Well, then, of course, the wedding couldn't be arranged and the whole business would start all over again. But the first thing that had to happen was that the parents had to choose. And how? How does one choose between one girl and another?"

"How?" I wanted to know.

"Let me tell you the story of Hannah and Reuben and you'll see. They were a happy couple, living in perfect harmony with their neighbors and their children. Hannah was the best of women, but she did have one failing. Her basket of wools resembled a nest of snakes. Every thread was twisted and knotted and tangled in with its neighbors, and each time poor

Hannah wished to embark upon a piece of darning, or start to knit a sock for her husband, she would be nearly weeping with frustration as she tried to separate off one color from another. It wasn't a basket of wools at all. What it was, was a 'plonter.' Well, Hannah and Reuben had a son, and it was time for this son to settle down with a wife. Hannah and Reuben employed a matchmaker to find him a suitable bride. Now this was all very good and fine for Hannah and Reuben and the matchmaker, who spent many a pleasant afternoon together, discussing the qualities of every single young lady of their acquaintance over cups of tea and biscuits flavored with almond essence and sprinkled with sugar. But Hannah and Reuben's son — let us call him Jacob — had other ideas. He wanted to marry his friend Rachel. They had grown up together and they loved each other.

One day, Jacob went to see his mother and father. They were alone, for once. He brought Rachel with him.

'Father, Mother, I would like you to know,' said Jacob, 'that I wish to marry Rachel.' "

"What did they say?" I asked. "Did they let him?"

"I'm glad," said my grandmother, "that you have never heard an argument such as went on there, in that house! There were shoutings, and cryings, and curses and threats and pleas, backwards and forwards and up and down for hours. Poor Rachel, forgotten during all this commotion between the parents and their child, sat at the table with Hannah's basket of wools in front of her. And as the storm of words and tears flew around her head, she began to unpick the knots in the wool, sort

out one color from another, untwist strands that had been twisted together for longer than anyone could remember, and wind the different colors into little skeins, shaped like small figures-of-eight. During a lull in the argument, Hannah glanced at her basket and saw that now her wools were lying curled up inside it in neat circles, all the colors singing out one after the other, distinct and beautiful, like summer flowers gathered in a vase.

'Reuben,' she said to her husband, 'I think we may have underestimated Rachel. Look at my wool basket.'

'You, my dear Hannah,' said Reuben, 'never had a wool basket. You had a mess. A "plonter." *That* is what I call a wool basket. Any woman who can sort out a tangle like the one created by my beloved wife with her threads is capable of great feats of patience and perseverance. Let this be a lesson to us, Hannah, my dear, not to overlook a treasure that is under our noses simply because we are used to it. Rachel, my dear, we would be honored if you would consider marrying our son.'"

"So did they marry and live happily ever after?" I asked. My grandmother laughed. "They married. Ever after I don't know about, but what I do know is that matchmakers, ever since that day, used to take a messy bundle of wools with them, and test out prospective brides. Any young woman who grew impatient and thrust the bundle from her in disgust had a couple of black marks written up against her name."

While my grandmother was telling me this story, I had been trying to make my own cross-stitches on a small piece of canvas. I was using wool and a long, silver needle, nearly as long as one of my fingers. I wanted my stitches to make the shape of a house, but when I looked down at my work, it didn't look like a house at all. Some of the walls were crooked and bulged outwards.

"Look," I said, almost crying, "it's horrible. It's not what it's supposed to be at all."

My grandmother looked. Then she took the work out of my hands and put it on the table.

"Let me tell you about the diamond," she said.

"Which diamond?"

"This was the largest and purest diamond in the world. It belonged to a great and powerful King. Now one day, a dreadful accident happened and the diamond was found to have a deep scratch in it. The King was more upset than he had ever been in his life. His perfect diamond was ruined forever. What was he to do?"

"What *did* he do?"

"He asked every jeweler he knew whether the gem could be polished to remove the scratch, and they were all agreed that it could not be done. The King was heartbroken, until one day, a jeweler arrived at the court from a far country, and asked to see the diamond.

'Give the jewel to me for a week,' said the stranger, 'and I will return it more beautiful than it was before.' Well, of course the King was overjoyed, but he couldn't allow the diamond out of his palace. Therefore he set the man to work in one of the rooms next to his own throne room, with two guards standing outside the door. When the week was over, the jeweler showed the

King what he had done. Using the deep scratch on the diamond to form the stem, he had carved a rose growing out of it, complete with leaves and petals and little rosebuds around it — all clearly cut into the jewel.

'You will be richly rewarded,' said the King, 'for improving on perfection.'

'The reward should not be for that,' answered the jeweler. 'But for taking a fault and transforming it into a virtue.'"

"I like the story," I said to my grandmother, "but what about my house?"

"It doesn't look like a house," said my grandmother. "It looks more like a face . . . so we'll turn the roof into a hat, and the windows into eyes, and we'll add a mouth smiling . . . and there you are."

And that is what we did.

SAVING THE PENNIES

IN my grandmother's bedroom, in the corner opposite the big brown cupboard, there stood an enormous wooden chest. The lid was too heavy for me to lift by myself, and my grandmother often said to me, "Never lift the lid of this chest on your own. If it were to fall on your fingers . . ." She would shake her

head then, as though she couldn't bear even to think of it. I was not interested in the contents of the chest. It was full of pillows and sheets and blankets and rolled-up quilts in embroidered white quilt covers.

"Why do we take all the pillows and blankets and put them away in the chest every morning?" I wanted to know. "It means that we have to make the beds again every night."

"It's not such a terrible thing, to make a bed," said my grandmother. "If we left the beds all ready, the whole apartment would look like a big dormitory. When my children were small, and my mother was still alive . . . ah, she was a wonderful woman. Have I ever told you about her?"

"Tell me again."

"We called her the Bobbeh. It means 'Grandmother.' Toward the end of her life, she became quite blind, but making all the beds at night, every night, was a task that she enjoyed. It took a long time. I had nine living children, remember. The Bobbeh used to take each pillow out of the chest and sniff it carefully. 'This one's Leah's,' she would say. 'This is Matilda's . . . and Sara's and Reuben's, and so on, sniffing every single one and putting it on the right bed. And she never, never made a mistake."

"Never?"

"Never. She was a remarkable woman."

Sometimes my grandmother wanted to clean the floor behind the chest, and Danny and I would help her pile all the bed linen onto one of the beds, and push the chest away from the corner. When it was empty, while my grandmother was busy cleaning the place where it had stood, Danny and I would climb into it and pretend it was a big brown boat that we were sailing across dangerous seas.

"If this chest had wheels," Danny said to my grandmother, "you could push us all over the room . . . all over the apartment. Then it really *would* be like a boat."

"Wheels on a chest!" said my grandmother. "That's all I need . . . a chance to spend my days pushing little children across the floor. It's a very good thing that chests are absolutely forbidden to have wheels."

"Forbidden?" I asked. "Who forbade it?"

"The Council of Wise Men in Chelm did."

"Oh, them!" I said. "They're not real. We don't have to listen to them. It's not *really* forbidden. Only in a story."

"Have you ever seen a chest with wheels?" asked my grand-mother.

"No, never," we said.

"Well, then. It shows that for once, the Council of Wise Men decided something correctly."

"But why did they?" I wanted to know. "Is there a story?"

"Certainly there's a story. The story of Chaim, the poor teacher, and his wife, Dvora. Take a pillow each to make the sitting a little softer and I'll tell you."

So Danny and I sat in the chest on two plump pillows and my grandmother told us the story.

"Many years ago, high up on a hill in Chelm, there lived a poor teacher called Chaim and his wife, Dvora. They were so poor that all they had to eat every day was bread with radishes.

Occasionally, an onion came their way. Dvora would take a few onion rings and boil them up with water and salt, throw in a couple of chicken feet that the butcher gave away because no one wanted them, and this mixture she would call 'soup.'

'The rich,' said Chaim, as he drank the colorless liquid from a spoon, 'have fluffy dumplings to go in their soup, made from matzo meal and chicken fat and egg, flavored with nutmeg and sprinkled with parsley. Their soup is yellow, the color of gold. One soup for the rich and one for the poor.' And he would sigh and dip his spoon into the bowl.

'When was the last time,' Dvora asked, 'that we tasted cake?' Chaim thought. 'Six months ago, at the wedding of the rabbi's daughter. Do you remember it?'

Dvora sighed. 'How could I forget it, a cake like that. Filled with chopped nuts and honey and apples, and sprinkled with cinnamon. Such a cake! A cake to dream about.'

Chaim pulled thoughtfully on his beard. 'Wife,' he said at last, 'I have a plan. A plan that will result in our very own cake.'

'Tell me,' said Dvora. 'A cake is what I would dearly like.'

'This is the plan. Do you remember my grandfather's big chest? The one on wheels? Well, we will make a small hole in the lid and lock the chest and give the key to a neighbor to keep. Then, every Friday, just before you light the Sabbath candles, you will put one penny into the chest. And every week before the Sabbath, I will put a penny in also. We are so poor that the loss of two pennies each week will make no difference to our wealth, but the pennies will add up, and in a year, or maybe even nine months, there will be enough in the chest to make the richest, tastiest cake in the whole history of Chelm.'

And so it was agreed. The very next Friday, Chaim put his penny into the chest. Before she lit the Sabbath candles, Dvora went to the chest and dropped her penny into it. Both Chaim and Dvora began to have dreams about the kind of cake it would be . . . Perhaps a plum cake? Or one with shavings of chocolate over the top? Thinking about the cake filled their minds every waking moment and for half the night as well.

By Thursday of the following week, however, Chaim had reached a decision. He was a teacher, and therefore a thinker, and his thoughts had been traveling along this path: 'If Dvora puts a penny in the chest every Friday, there will easily be enough pennies after a year to make a perfectly adequate cake. Why should I waste my penny (which Heaven knows I'm desperately in need of) when Dvora's penny will be quite sufficient? No, I will keep my money and say not a word to Dvora and spend it on something else . . . something I need now.' So Chaim went off to the synagogue that Friday without putting anything into the chest, and continued putting nothing in it, week after week after week.

Meanwhile Dvora (who had the day-to-day cooking to do, don't forget) said to herself: 'I have little enough money to spend as it is. Why should I make myself poorer when Chaim is putting in quite enough money for both of us? After all, what does it matter if the cake is a little smaller, a little less rich? To us, it will still taste like Paradise. No, I will keep my penny and say not a word to Chaim, and try and find a marrow bone for proper soup for once.' So she stopped putting her pennies into the chest. Well, the weeks passed and the months passed and when springtime came, Dvora said: 'It's April, Chaim. Nearly a year since we started collecting money for our cake. Let us go and open the chest and count the pennies and plan our wonderful treat.'

Dvora went to fetch the key from the neighbor and together husband and wife approached the chest. Chaim bent to unlock it. As he opened the lid, Dvora started screaming: 'Oh, Chaim, Chaim, we've been robbed! Look! There are only two pennies left! Oh, who could have done such a wicked thing?' Now Chaim was not clever (because everyone in Chelm is a fool, do you remember?), but he *was* a teacher and therefore could at least put two and two together.

'Don't be silly!' he said to Dvora. 'How could anyone have taken our money? Did you not see me with your own eyes unlock the chest, not half a minute ago? No, I accuse you, wife, of not being honest. I say you have tricked me! You have not been putting in your penny every week, have you?'

Dvora covered her face with her apron and started crying. '*I* have tricked you? Oh, you monster! How can you accuse me when you are the scoundrel? How? *You* have never put a penny in the chest either. And now we've got nothing. No pennies and no cake and almost a whole year gone.' She dropped her apron, and began to shake her husband until his teeth rattled. He snarled at her, and the long and the short of it was, they both fell into the chest, and the lid slammed down on top of them and snapped tight shut. Well, then, Chaim and Dvora began to push and struggle to get out like two kittens in a pillowcase, and the

violent movement set the wheels of the chest rolling, and it rolled right out of the house and down the hill into the main street. As you can imagine, the citizens of Chelm had no idea what was happening. There they were, quietly minding their business, when suddenly, along came a huge wooden contraption, careering toward them, ready to crush them to pulp. And not only that, dreadful screams and shrieks were coming from the inside of the chest, so that half the people of Chelm were convinced that all the devils of Hell were bundled up in there, and ran away in one direction, while the other half (composed mainly of children and dogs) chased after the chest, adding their cries to the ones issuing from within its wooden depths. In the end the chest stopped rolling right in front of the synagogue. The Chief Sage (yes, wearing his golden shoes on his hands!) came out and quickly sent for a locksmith.

When the locksmith opened the chest and Chaim and Dvora popped out, all disheveled and with their clothes torn and dusty, everyone stepped back in amazement. The Council of Wise Men listened to what the teacher and his wife had to say and the Chief Sage invited them both to his house for the evening, because it just so happened that his wife had baked a cake that day. Two important laws were passed in Chelm shortly after that. The first was that no teacher should ever live at the top of a hill, and the second law was that from that day to this, no chest is allowed to have wheels on it. Now jump out of there, both of you, and help me to push this boat of yours back into the corner."

THE GARDEN OF TALKING FLOWERS

MY grandmother's apartment had no garden, but on the balcony at the front of the building she kept a collection of small, reddish-brown flowerpots with spiky cacti growing in them. There were also two bigger earthenware tubs, overflowing with geraniums. Watering the flowerpots was one of the tasks I enjoyed best. My grandmother would fill a jug with water, and I would carry it out of the kitchen and carefully around two sides of the table in the dining room and out onto the balcony. The earth around each cactus was cracked and dry and almost the same color as the flowerpots, but as soon as I poured some water onto it from my jug, it became a wonderful, dark shiny brown, like melted chocolate, and all the little cracks would disappear. I enjoyed pouring water so much that sometimes the soil round the plants couldn't soak it up fast enough and it came out of the bottom of the pot and spread over the pale yellow tiles of the balcony floor. These tiles had flower patterns cut into them, and my grandmother never minded them getting wet, because the sun dried them almost at once. I liked pouring water on the tiles. From being butter-yellow, they turned khaki-color when they were wet, and I always felt that it was only fair to give some nourishment to the poor thirsty flower shapes cut into the stone.

A real garden was something we only saw on walks around the city. We'd go down the hill and turn left, and along narrow streets where the houses almost seemed to meet above our heads. We looked into courtyards as we passed, to see what people were growing. In one house, the families had turned the courtyard into a small garden with trees and flowers blooming right in the middle of the building. On our walks we would see avenues of pepper trees, and hedges heavy with pale blue plumbago flowers, and everywhere we could smell the fragrance of pine trees. There was an almond tree outside

Genzel's shop, looking out of place on the gray pavement.

"They built the houses and the streets around it," my grand-mother said, "and now everyone looks at it as the winter ends, and waits for the pink and white blossoms to tell them spring is here. The almond tree always blooms for the festival of Tu B'Shvat." She sang me the song:

"The almond tree in flower,
The bright sun in the sky,
Birds up on the highest roof
Sing that Tu B'Shvat is nigh.

Tu B'Shvat is here now,
Almond blossom time!
Tu B'Shvat is here now,
Almond blossom time!"

A little way away from my grandmother's apartment, across the road and on the corner of the next street, was Moshe's flower shop. Whenever we went visiting, my grandmother would go into this shop and gather a bunch of flowers. Moshe or his wife, Mazal, would walk about with us, in and out of the giant vases standing on the floor, while we chose what we wanted: pale pink gladioli, perhaps, so tall that they seemed to me like thin tree branches waving above my head, or red carnations, or the tightly curled-up buds of yellow roses. I loved to watch Moshe take the flowers and wrap them in whispery sheets of paper and tie a beautiful ribbon around the stems. The shop smelled green and moist. It smelled of earth and moss and fern and hundreds and hundreds of flowers. In summer, Moshe kept the shutters closed to protect the flowers from the sun, and stepping into the shop was like entering a cool, dark cave.

My grandmother took a bunch of flowers with her when she went out for a visit, and many people who came to the apartment brought her flowers. She never arranged them while the visitors were still there, but as soon as they'd gone, she would take out the vases and put the flowers in, one by one, and I would help her.

"Which do you like best," I asked one day, "carnations or gladioli or roses?"

"Why do I have to like one best?" asked my grandmother. "Can't I like them all? It reminds me of a story."

"What story?"

"A story about a garden. Sit there while I put these flowers in water and I'll tell it to you."

"Was it a big garden? What did it have growing in it?"

"This garden," said my grandmother, "was the biggest and most beautiful garden in the whole history of the world. Not since Adam and Eve were banished from Paradise has there been such a garden. In it grew every kind of flower from the daisy to the rose. There were fountains and peacocks and trellises and terraces and arbors and benches and streams and trees of every description: noble cedars, slender cypresses, flowering almonds, and orchards and orchards of fruit trees. This was a garden as large as a city. No one knew who owned it, but whoever it was must have been extraordinarily rich and powerful, because not only was this garden magnificent, it was also magical."

"Magical?" I asked. "How was it magical?"

"Because," said my grandmother, "every single plant and creature in this garden could talk."

"Wonderful!" I said.

"Well, it was wonderful in one way and in another, it caused a great deal of trouble. The reason it caused trouble was this: As the plants and flowers had nothing better to do, they began to boast, each one saying how beautiful she was, and how much better she was than her neighbor. The air, as well as being filled with the fragrance of the flowers, was also, alas, filled with their voices.

'Look at me,' said the poppy. 'My petals are much more delicate than anyone else's and no one can match my scarlet.'

'But your petals tear so easily,' remarked the oleander. 'Just one puff of wind and you're in tatters.'

'That's a typically poisonous remark,' sniffed an orchid that looked very like a small dragon, 'from a poisonous flower. Quite what I'd expect.'

'No need to get agitated,' said the lofty gladiolus in a languid tone. 'I can't imagine anyone being preferred to me. See the economical way that I arrange my flowers all along my stem? And there are so many of them!'

'Some plants,' whispered one carnation to another, 'try to dazzle us with their quantity in the hope that we will not remark upon their quality.'

'Quite so,' answered the second carnation. 'And it would be hard to find a better-quality flower than us: such a range of colors, such fragrance, such frilly petals and so long-lasting. Is it any wonder we are so often chosen for boutonnieres?'

'I,' said the pale lily, 'would be mortified if I were chosen as a boutonniere. I am elegance and purity itself. I have been told so, often.'

'No one even notices us,' muttered the daisies, 'making the grass look pretty day after day, getting trodden on all the time with not so much as a word of apology. People don't even think of us as proper flowers.'

The rose smiled. 'You may all chatter and quarrel among yourselves. We know, and anyone who knows anything at all knows, that the rose is the queen of any garden. As far as I'm concerned, there's nothing to discuss.'

The trees growing in the garden heard the flowers bickering among themselves.

'Those flowers,' murmured the pine tree. 'I don't know why they give themselves such airs. They grow, they are cut down, they die. We trees, on the other hand, are useful. We provide shelter for birds and animals, we live almost forever. We give fruit year after year, and when we are cut down, the wood from our trunks and branches makes houses where people can live.'

'We should have a contest,' said the willow tree, 'to see which of all the plants in the garden is the very best.'

'But who will judge the contest?' whispered the cedar.

'I will,' said the dove. 'I will fly through the length and breadth of the garden and look at every flower, tree, and shrub, and then I will give my judgment.'

The trees agreed and rustled the message on to the flowers, who became very excited at the thought of a contest. It was to

take place on the very next Thursday afternoon. All the flowers preened themselves and made an effort to put out their newest, freshest buds on Thursday morning. The trees arranged their leaves to the best advantage, and urged birds to spring-clean their nests for the occasion. On Thursday morning, the dove flew for the last time through the garden, noticing the curling petals of the peony, the wax-white flowers on the camellia, and the weight of blossom on the branches of the apricot tree . . . and noticing also one tree that stood apart from the others, its trunk old and twisted, its leaves a dull grayish green, its roots in rocky soil. The dove fluttered round this tree and came to rest on one of its branches.

'Trees and flowers of this wonderful garden,' said the dove. 'Listen to me. I have made my judgment. I have flown around and around this place, looking at everything. It is true that the rose is the most beautiful of the flowers.'

'There, what did I tell you?' said the rose in a loud whisper, her stem bending graciously this way and that, her face elegantly framed by new green leaves.

'But,' the dove went on, 'the rose pricks the fingers of those who try to pluck her, and so in the end, I decided to award the greatest honor to a tree.'

'Which tree? Which tree?' murmured every leaf in the garden.

'Why, this very tree that I am sitting on now,' said the dove. 'The olive tree.'

None of the other trees could understand it. The olive tree was old and twisted. Its leaves were dull. How could it possibly compare with the dignity of the cedar, the elegance of the cypress, the beauty of the willow?

'I will explain to you all,' said the dove, 'why I have chosen the olive tree. There are four reasons. Firstly, because its fruit, unlike the fruit of the apple, the pear, the plum, and the apricot, is salty and sharp and when pressed, yields a nourishing and fragrant oil. Secondly, because the olive does not flaunt its beautiful wood, but hides it under a rough bark. Thirdly, because the olive gives its fruit willingly, even though it is shaken and beaten with sticks, and lastly, because God's own dove chose an olive branch to take to Noah to show him that the flood was at an end. The olive tree therefore combines usefulness and beauty, modesty and kindness and is a symbol of peace in the world. I could choose no other.'

All the trees were silent after the dove's judgment. The flowers, too, had to agree that what the dove said had been very sensible. Only the rose still thought she should have been chosen, but she kept her thoughts to herself and harmony was restored to the garden."

THE MARKET OF MISERIES

EVERY week, my grandmother spent the whole of Friday preparing for the Sabbath, the day of rest when no cooking could be done and when work of every kind was forbidden. The Sabbath began on Friday at dusk and ended on Saturday, as soon as three stars became visible in the sky.

There were rules in my grandmother's kitchen, and everyone had to follow them.

"It's a kosher kitchen," she explained to me. "Everything is done according to very ancient laws. I have two sets of everything: knives, forks, plates, pots, and pans. One set is for dishes cooked with meat, and the other for dishes with milk in them. Milk and meat must never be mixed." I did not understand exactly why these rules were important, but I was careful, when I dried the knives and forks, to use the towel with the red stripe across it for the meat things, and the one with the blue stripe for milk dishes.

I enjoyed all the preparations. In the kitchen, there was the food to cook, and once that was done, it had to be packed very carefully into a large, square metal tin that sat on top of a little stove, which burned with a tiny blue flame, all through Friday night and for most of Saturday.

I used to help my grandmother with the food. Because I wasn't allowed near the frying pan, I sat at the kitchen table and dipped pearly slices of fish first into beaten egg, then into matzo meal, ready for my grandmother to cook. The pieces of fish made a loud hissing noise as they touched the hot oil, and pale blue smoke rose up and up and disappeared before it reached the ceiling. Another task I was allowed to help with was packing the eggs. I had to shell about a dozen hard-boiled eggs and put them carefully into a dish. This dish had a cover that fitted tightly over the top. When the eggs went in on Friday, they were white with clear yellow yolks, just as you would expect, but as if by magic, when we took them out on Saturday, the whites were the color of coffee with cream in it, and the yolks had turned into small moons: pale, pale yellow edged with a bluish gray.

"It's from standing all night long and cooking," my grandmother explained, but I still believed it was magic. Nothing else that cooked all night changed color. The largest pot of all contained the cholent: a stew made with beans and potatoes and meat that was so tender when you ate it that it fell into soft strands in your mouth and sometimes became stuck between your teeth. Then there were flasks of tea and coffee, and airtight tins full of strudel and cinnamon biscuits, and of course, the kugel.

There was another kitchen task I liked, although I never did it on a Friday, and that was cleaning the rice. My grandmother would shake the rice out of a big, brown paper bag onto a round brass tray, and spread it out for me, so that it covered all the curly patterns of leaves and flowers scratched onto the metal. The rice made a thin hard sound as it fell onto the tray, like the sound of hailstones bouncing off a window. I had to push the grains around with my fingers and find the horrible blackened ones, and remove them to a little plate my grandmother put next to the tray.

It was fortunate that the Sabbath was a day for visits, because otherwise I would have been very bored indeed. No sewing or writing was allowed, and I was too young to be able to read. What I did was listen. My grandmother's friends would sit and drink tea and eat biscuits and strudel, and talk and talk. Their talk, if I understood it at all, seemed to me to be mainly complaints: about their husbands, children, about shopkeepers, about life in general. I said so to my grandmother.

"Everyone enjoys a good 'kvetch' now and then," she said.

"What's a kvetch?" I wanted to know.

"A complaint. A moan. A kvetch is also the name for some-one who whines. I'll tell you a story about a kvetch. Listen. Once upon a time, long ago, there lived a woman called Zilpa. She was married and had two children, a son and a daughter. She had a sister and a mother-in-law. She had two friends called Mina and Rina. And all she did, all day long, from morning till night, was complain.

'My husband never listens to me,' she would say. 'He sits all day long with his head in a book and if I speak to him he either nods or grunts or both. Oh, how I wish I could have a more attentive husband. Can there be a more annoying characteristic in a man?'

Then she would complain about her son. 'Lazy? I never saw anything like it in my life. Why, if he could manage to go to school lying down, then he would. Why do other mothers have such diligent, hard-working sons, when I am saddled with a slug-a-bed?'

When she had finished on the subject of her son, Zilpa would go on to her daughter. 'God has given me an untidy daughter. She will never marry, and if she does, her husband will divorce her in a week, she is so messy. Why, the other day I went into her room and it took me half an hour to find the door again, such a dreadful upheaval there was in there.'

On the subject of her mother-in-law, she was at her loudest. 'Nothing I do for her son is good enough! Why is it I who have to suffer such a persnickety creature for a mother-in-law? Why is it not my sister? Oh, no, she has all the luck. Her mother-in-law hardly dares to open her mouth, let alone criticize. And while I think of my sister, why does she live in such a fine house on the fashionable side of town, while I survive in this hovel with my inattentive husband, lazy son, messy daughter, and carping mother-in-law?'

You are probably wondering who Zilpa was complaining to when she spoke in this way about the various members of her family. The answer is: to her friends, Mina and Rina. What else are friends for, if not to listen to a person's innermost kvetches? But naturally (once a kvetch, always a kvetch!), moaning to Mina and Rina did not prevent Zilpa from telling her family a few home truths about her friends.

'That Mina,' she would say to her mother-in-law, 'she never invites us to her house . . . never. Sits and drinks gallons of tea in my house, and eats her own weight in sugared almonds, but will she invite us to her house? When the Messiah comes, maybe. And Rina never stops talking, not even to draw breath. My this . . . my that . . . never a word about anyone else's concerns. And you wouldn't believe some of the things she says about people! It wouldn't surprise me at all if she spreads wicked lies about me. It's no more than I would expect.'

And so, Zilpa's life went on — one long, unending, never-changing kvetch. The noise of her complaints grew and grew, until at last it reached the ears of the Angels in Heaven.

'Go to that woman,' said the Chief Angel to one of the Lesser Angels, 'and direct her to the Market of Miseries.' So the Lesser Angel took on the shape of a peddler and called on Zilpa one morning.

'I don't know what you think you're going to sell me,' said Zilpa. 'I haven't a penny to spare. Nothing ever goes right for me. Other women manage to have enough money to buy a length of ribbon if it takes their fancy, but not me, oh no. I'm sorry. You've come to the wrong house.'

'I can see,' said the Angel, who was as clever as all angels are, 'that you are an extremely unfortunate lady. Someone as intelligent and charming as you are shouldn't have to be worried about money.'

Zilpa thought: What a delightful man! How rare to come across someone so understanding! She said, 'It's not only the money, you know. There's my inattentive husband, my lazy son, my messy daughter, my persnickety mother-in-law and my unsatisfactory friends.'

'Tsk! Tsk!' said the Angel-peddler. 'It seems to me that you should pay a visit to the Market of Miseries.'

'The Market of Miseries?' said Zilpa. 'I've never heard of it.'

'I would have to take you there,' said the peddler with a smile. 'It is, of course, not open to everyone. Only to very special, worthy people.'

'Goodness!' said Zilpa. 'It sounds very interesting. Will it take long? To get there, I mean, and to come back?'

'Not long at all,' said the peddler. 'It is twelve o'clock now. We will be back before you can blink.' That, Zilpa thought, was probably an exaggeration. She took off her apron, picked up her basket, and called out to her husband, who was in the house:

'I'm going to the market! Back in an hour.'

'Mmmm,' said her husband from deep in the house.

'Do you see what I mean?' Zilpa asked the peddler.

'Indeed. Follow me,' said the peddler, and began to walk away from Zilpa's front door. She walked behind him. The streets of the city, the streets she recognized, soon gave way to a rough track that wound between fields studded with boulders. The Angel-peddler and Zilpa walked and walked.

This market, Zilpa was thinking, is very far away. I will never be back before one o'clock. And there's nobody here . . . not anywhere. Who has ever heard of a market with no people? I should never have followed this man. Perhaps he will kill me and leave my body by the side of the road. And Zilpa began to tremble.

'Here we are,' said the peddler, and pointed into the distance. Yes, Zilpa thought, I can see something . . . perhaps the outskirts of another town. Yes, yes, there are awnings flapping . . . people . . . market stalls . . . oh, how marvelous!

The peddler turned to her. 'You have complained about your husband, your children, your sister, your mother-in-law, and your friends. Therefore, you may walk about wherever you wish in this market, and choose other faults for all of them . . . and then they will cease to be as they are and will be as you wish them to be.'

'Thank you,' said Zilpa, and began to walk about among the stalls.

'Husband?' said the first stall holder, who was dressed in red from head to toe, with a red veil hiding her face. 'I can offer you cruelty, drunkenness, ignorance, meanness, a love of gambling, infidelity, violence, lack of humor, or inattentiveness.'

'Oh, my word!' said Zilpa. 'I've never thought about it before. I suppose, out of all those, inattentiveness is the best.'

'I'll wrap it up for you,' said the veiled stall holder, and she put a small parcel into Zilpa's basket.

The next stall holder was dressed in blue, and veiled like her neighbor. 'Children's faults!' she called out. 'Come and choose! Lovely wide variety! Dishonesty, stupidity, dislike of parents, a longing to leave home, rages, sulking, laziness, messiness . . . all bargains . . . come and choose.'

'I suppose,' said Zilpa, 'laziness and messiness, please.' Two more small parcels found their way into Zilpa's basket.

'Sisters?' said the next stall holder, dressed from head to toe in yellow, with yellow veils over her face. 'You can have them envious, spiteful, flirtatious, two-faced, unkind, luckier than you are . . .'

Zilpa sighed. 'What can I say? Luckier than me, I suppose.'

'Here you are, then,' said the yellow-draped figure, and another parcel was added to those in Zilpa's basket. The stall holder in the mother-in-law stall was wearing green. 'Can I tempt you?' she said. 'Jealousy, ill health, drunkenness, idleness, extravagance, lying, a sharp tongue, fussiness. The choice is yours.'

'Fussiness, please,' said Zilpa. Her basket was nearly full now. Only the stall for friends was left for her to visit.

The stall holder said, from behind her purple veil:

'Spitefulness, envy, betrayal, meanness, gossiping, ill-wishing, tale bearing, visiting too often and not inviting you back . . .'

'I'll have visiting too often, and gossiping,' said Zilpa.

The Angel-peddler appeared suddenly at Zilpa's side.

'Are you ready?' he said. 'There is only one more stall to visit. It's the place where you may pick a Supplementary Misery, if you wish. Or not, if you choose not to.'

'What are they, these supplementary miseries?'

'All sorts of things . . . assorted ailments from pimples to the plague, hunger, pain, poverty, war, anguish. On a good day, one can even find Death.'

'No, no,' said Zilpa. 'Thank you very much. I'm very satisfied with what I've got. I won't be needing any supplementary miseries.'

'Very well,' said the peddler. 'Then I shall take you home.'

Before Zilpa could say another word, there she was, back in her own courtyard. The peddler was nowhere to be seen. She glanced down at her basket, and was astonished to see, instead of the miseries she had collected in the market, seven ripe pomegranates. She went into the house and looked at the clock.

'It must have stopped,' she said to herself. 'It still says twelve o'clock.' But the clock was ticking loudly.

'I've just been to the market,' said Zilpa to her husband, who looked up and smiled.

'You told me that just a moment ago,' he said. 'I expect you thought I wasn't listening, as usual. You also told me it took an hour.'

Zilpa was just about to correct her husband, when she stopped herself. Better to say nothing, she thought. I must have been dreaming. She went into the kitchen to put the pomegranates away, and the peddler returned to the Gates of

Heaven, where he was welcomed by all the other angels.

'It never fails,' said the Chief Angel. 'Never. When people have a chance of choosing their misfortunes, out of all the available shapes and sizes of miseries offered to them, they always, always choose the ones they already know: their own.'

And all the angels laughed heartily at human beings, and at how predictable they were."

AN OVERCROWDED HOUSE

IN the entrance hall of my grandmother's apartment, there was a cupboard set so high up in the wall that only a tall person standing on a chair could open it. Luckily, my grandmother needed what was kept up there once a year only, so it had to be reached on two occasions: once, to bring out the Passover dishes ready for the Festival, every spring, and the second time to put them all away for another twelve months. My tallest cousin, Arieh, was always the person who had to stand on the chair and pass down dishes and cups and plates, knives and forks and pots and pans and glasses to my grandmother and me, waiting to carry them to the kitchen.

At Passover time, all the ordinary dishes were put away and the whole apartment was cleaned from top to bottom. Not a single crumb was allowed to lurk forgotten in the corner. Holes in the wall had to be plastered over. Sometimes, my grandmother decided that this or that room needed whitewashing, and she would pile all the furniture into the middle of the room for a day, and cover it with sheets, and then slap a thick, white sloppy brush up and down the walls.

"Why do you have the best things hidden away in the cupboard all the time?" I asked my grandmother. "Why are they only allowed down into the house for a week?"

"Because it's a special celebration," said my grandmother. "It's to celebrate the escape of the Jews from their captivity in Egypt. We will read the whole story again, on the night of the First Seder."

For the Seder the door between the dining room and the room where the long, blue sofa was, was folded back, and the table was pulled out to its full length. More than twenty people would sit around it for the Passover meal, eating matzos and bitter herbs and drinking sweet wine, and telling the story of the Plagues that God sent down to the land of Egypt. In the Hagadah, the book we looked at as the meal continued, there were colored drawings of the Plagues: frogs, locusts, boils, and a very frightening picture showing a dead child covered in blood, and representing the Death of the First Born. There was also a picture of Moses parting the Red Sea, with high, blue waves towering above the heads of the Israelites like walls of sapphire. We sang songs, and waited up till late at night to see whether this year, the prophet Elijah would come and drink the glass of wine my grandmother always put out for him. At the end of the meal, my cousins and I would run all over the apartment searching for the Afikoman. This was half a matzo, wrapped in a napkin, which my grandmother hid like a treasure. Whoever found it won a small prize: an apple or a square of chocolate. There were so many cousins rushing about that I never managed to find the Afikoman, but my grandmother gave us all apples and chocolate too, so I didn't mind.

"It's not very fair for the winner, though," I said to my grandmother. "It makes winning less special."

"Nonsense," said my grandmother. "Finding the Afikoman is an honor and it brings good luck. And looking all over the place is fun too."

In spite of the special dishes, and the book with pictures of the Plagues, in spite of the sips of sweet wine and the brown-freckled matzos which tasted so delicious with strawberry jam on them, I was always quite glad when the festival was over and the visitors went home. Then I could have my grandmother to myself again and she could tell me stories.

"You don't know," she said, "how well off you are. I should tell you the story of Mordechai and Chaya. Once upon a time, there was a farmer called Mordechai, who lived in a miserable little farmhouse right on the edge of the village. He had two muddy fields next to the house, where he tried to grow this and that and the other. I have to tell you that most of the time he failed miserably, and when Chaya took the farm produce to the market and set it out on a stall, people walked by with their noses in the air saying, 'Pshaw! Such cabbages I wouldn't feed to my chickens! Do you call this a turnip? This is a turnip's wizened grandfather! And this is not a potato, this is a joke,' and so forth. But Chaya didn't laugh. The money grew scarcer and scarcer, and the couple grew more and more miserable. Then, one terrible day, Mordechai's father died, leaving Mordechai's mother penniless. She had to sell her house to pay her late husband's debts, and so there she was, homeless at her age. Well, there was no alternative: the poor old lady had to move in at once with Mordechai and Chaya. It was difficult to know quite where to put her. The farmhouse was really two rooms: one large room, with a corner curtained off to hide the bed where Mordechai and Chaya slept, and one tiny room that the couple called the kitchen, but which could more accurately have been called a cupboard with a window. When Mordechai's mother moved in, he hung a curtain across another corner of the large room, to hide the bed she had brought with her, and tried to make the best of it. But it was difficult.

'What shall we do?' he asked Chaya. 'She snores at night and keeps me awake.'

'She squeezes into the kitchen to help me cook,' said Chaya, 'so that I can hardly move. I think you should go and see the Rabbi. Ask his advice.'

'What good will that do?' asked Mordechai.

'What harm will it do?' his wife replied.

So in the end, Mordechai went to the Rabbi and told him all his troubles. This rabbi was not as clever as Rabbi Samuels, but he wasn't a fool. He listened to Mordechai, and muttered and mumbled into his beard, and fixed his eyes on an interesting spot on the ceiling, and finally he turned to Mordechai.

'Have you any livestock?' he asked.

'A few chickens . . . a goat . . . a cow to give milk . . . nothing much, I assure you.'

'Take the chickens,' said the Rabbi, 'and move them into the house with you.'

'Into the house?' Mordechai thought the Rabbi had gone mad.

'Exactly,' said the Rabbi, 'do as I say and your troubles will soon be over.'

Mordechai did as the Rabbi said. Never had he and Chaya been so miserable. The chickens squawked all day and got under everyone's feet. They laid eggs in unexpected places and flew onto the table at mealtimes to share what little food there was. The rooster had decided that Mordechai and Chaya's brass bedstead was his perch, and there every morning he would split the dawn in half with his crowing. Mordechai and Chaya used to leap out of their skins in fright.

'Go back to the Rabbi,' said Chaya. 'Tell him everything is ten times worse than before.'

So Mordechai went and poured out all his woes to the Rabbi. The Rabbi muttered and mumbled into his beard and fixed his eyes on an interesting spot on the back of the door, and then finally he turned to Mordechai.

'You said you had a cow?' he asked.

'Yes . . . one cow.'

'Bring the cow into the house,' said the Rabbi.

'Where will I put her?'

'Tie her up to the handle of the door,' said the Rabbi. 'All your troubles will soon be over.'

Mordechai returned to the farmhouse and told his wife what the Rabbi had said.

'He has taken leave of his senses,' said Chaya. 'But he is an educated man, so we should at least try it.'

Life immediately went from bad to worse. No one could move in or out of the door without bumping into the cow. Twice, she pulled the rickety door off its hinges, and once chewed up both the curtain hiding Mordechai's mother's bed and some of her blankets as well.

'Go back to the Rabbi,' said Chaya after a week had passed. 'Tell him everything is a hundred times worse than before.'

So Mordechai went and cried out his anguish to the Rabbi. The Rabbi muttered and mumbled into his beard and fixed his eyes on an interesting spot on the floor and then finally he turned to Mordechai.

'Do you still have a goat?'

'Yes . . . one goat.'

'Bring the goat into the house.'

'Where will I put him?'

'Tie him up to the end of your bed,' said the Rabbi, 'and your troubles will soon be over.'

Mordechai returned to the farmhouse. When he told Chaya what the Rabbi had said, she couldn't believe her ears.

'The Rabbi is bewitched,' she cried. 'What is he telling us to do? Look at my house. Look what he has made us do already.

There are chickens wherever you look, clucking and squawking and dropping eggs and feathers all over the floor, the cow knocks over all the furniture and pulls the door off its hinges, my linen drawer has become a manger full of straw, and now he wants us to bring in the goat as well . . . and tie him to the end of our bed. It's too much!' She sat down at the table and wept salty tears into the dough she had been kneading.

'But you said yourself,' said Mordechai, 'he is an educated man, and so we should at least try it.' So Chaya wiped her tears away and went to fetch the goat.

The next day, Chaya went with Mordechai to see the Rabbi. They sat at the table and Chaya spoke first.

'My husband has been to you before,' she said, 'and you have advised him and we have followed your advice. Yesterday you told us to bring in the goat, and we did it, and today we are both three-quarters of the way to our graves. It wasn't the fact that the goat ate every single thing it could reach, including a piece from my husband's nightshirt. After all, what do I own that's too precious for a goat to eat? Nothing, that's what. No, Rabbi, what finally drove us to seek your help is the stench. Have you ever slept within three feet of a goat? I thought my last hour had come. We have not slept a wink all night. Tell us, Rabbi, what do we do now?'

The Rabbi did not mutter, nor did he mumble. He did not fix his eyes on interesting spots anywhere in the room. Instead, he spoke straight to Mordechai and Chaya.

'Take the goat and the cow and the chickens out of your house. Return them to their own quarters. Then clean your house from top to bottom, and come and tell me how you feel.'

Two days later, Mordechai and Chaya returned to the Rabbi's house.

'Oh, thank you, thank you, Rabbi,' they said. 'Our house is restored to us. It is clean and quiet and it doesn't smell of goat!'

'But what about Mordechai's mother? Do you not find it crowded?' said the Rabbi.

'Crowded?' said Mordechai. 'It's like a palace.'

'Paradise!' agreed Chaya. 'I shall never complain about it ever again.'

And she never did."

A Phantom at the Wedding

ALL sorts of people came to visit my grandmother. The most frequent visitors were members of the family: her sons and daughters and her grandchildren, her brother, his children and their children, and representatives of other, more distant branches of the family tree.

Then there were my grandmother's friends. I liked it when these ladies came to call because they generally wore necklaces and brooches that twinkled and glittered against the navy blue,

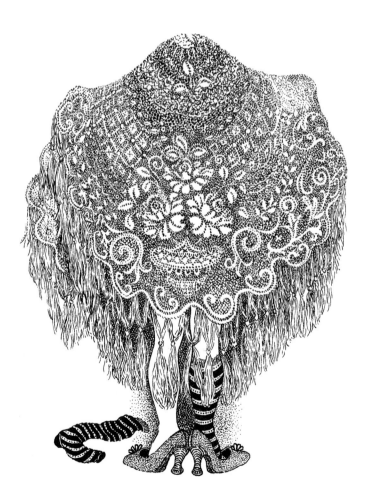

or olive green, or brown or black of their dresses. They would kiss me and feel my hair and hug me close to their bosoms till I could smell the sugary fragrance of their face powder. If I admired their jewels, they would take them off at once, and pin them on me or drape them around my neck, and I would run off to the shoe cupboard and put on a pair of my aunt Sara's shoes, just to complete the magnificence of my outfit. These ladies drank tea and ate cake and talked to my grandmother about their children and their grandchildren and listened to her stories, but sometimes there was another kind of visitor to the apartment.

The bell would ring and I would go and open the door — only to find a ragged old man with a wispy gray beard standing there, looking at me from under the brim of a black felt hat. My grandmother had several men like this who came ringing at the door, and they were all old and all had wispy white beards and wore black hats and long black coats that nearly touched the floor. They would shuffle into the dining room and sit muttering to my grandmother in Yiddish for a while, and then they would go shuffling away again. They never ate or drank anything while they were in the apartment. I asked my grandmother once who they were.

"They are Jews who do not have enough money. All they do all day is study the word of God, and then sometimes they come and collect money from richer people, people like us."

"Don't they earn money, for reading about God all day?"

"Not very much, I'm afraid. So they collect from various houses, and giving them charity is a duty and a blessing."

"Have you got enough money to give some to all of them?" I wanted to know. "Will there be enough left for us?" My grandmother laughed. "Of course! And in any case, no one should have too much money. It's bad for you, like too much food."

"Bad for you?" I was amazed. "How can it be bad for you? If you had a lot of money, you could have anything you liked."

"But too much money makes you extremely selfish. Look, I'll show you, just in the way that one of the ancient Rabbis showed a miser about selfishness, long ago. Go and look out the window."

I went and looked down into the street.

"What can you see?" asked my grandmother.

"The street . . . cars . . . the Eiges's apartment. Someone is beating a carpet . . . Moshe and Mazal's shop . . . Genzel's . . ."

"What else?"

"People walking about."

"Exactly," said my grandmother. "How many people?"

"A lot . . . two men. A woman and a dog. A group of children . . . some big, some little . . . All kinds of people."

"Now touch the window." I touched it. "What is it made of?" she continued.

"It's made of glass," I said.

"Quite right. Now come with me to the bedroom." I followed her down the corridor and stood in front of the mirrored panel of the big, brown cupboard.

"What can you see now?" asked my grandmother.

"I can see myself."

"Just you?"

"Just me."

"Now touch the mirror," said my grandmother. "What is it made of?"

"I think it's made of glass," I said.

"You're right. It *is* made of glass, exactly like the glass in the window, which you touched a moment ago. But what do you suppose has happened to this glass? Why can't you see anything except yourself?"

I shook my head. "Why?" I asked. "I don't know."

"Because," said my grandmother, "the back of the glass is coated with silver . . . the same silver that money is made from. The ancient Rabbi told the miser that it was silver and nothing but silver which made him see only himself, and which prevented him from seeing other people, and therefore stopped him from thinking about their welfare."

"Thank you for the story," I said, "but why do those old men never have a cup of tea or a biscuit while they're here?"

"Oh, they're much too devout," said my grandmother. "Even though I keep a strict division in my kitchen between meat dishes and milk dishes, they don't know me well enough to be sure of that, you see, and rather than risk eating something unclean by mistake, they eat and drink nothing at all."

I looked at the closed doors of the big, brown cupboard, then at my grandmother.

"Please may I take out the shawls?" I asked. This was a very special treat. My grandmother kept her shawls on the top shelf. They were beautifully knitted in pale colors and soft wool; lacy, filmy triangles and squares that she wrapped around her shoulders as she sat on the balcony on cool evenings.

"But be careful with them," she said as she brought them down for me. "Don't get the wool caught on anything. What are you going to be today? A princess?"

"A bride," I answered, choosing a huge, white shawl and covering my head with it.

"Can you breathe under there?" asked my grandmother.

"The lace is full of holes," I said. "I can see the whole room with a pattern of white leaves and flowers over it."

"Tell me when the wedding is over," said my grandmother, "and I will tell you a story about a bride."

"Tell it to me now," I said, "and I'll play later."

My grandmother sighed. "Very well, but at least take the shawl off your face while you listen."

So I took the shawl from over my head and put it around my shoulders as I listened to my grandmother.

"This," she said, "is a story about a ghost. Do you like stories like that?"

"Is it very frightening?"

"No, not very frightening. Perhaps touching would be a better word. Do you remember my aunt Nehama?"

I nodded. I remembered her well. Aunt Nehama was the oldest person I had ever seen. Her face was lined and creased all over, like a walnut, and her hands were brown and stiff and covered in lumps and bumps: they looked like the twisted roots of a tree. Aunt Nehama never moved. She sat in her house in a high-backed chair at the kitchen table, drinking black coffee and smoking dark yellow cigarettes. She had a black scarf tied around her head. I had been quite glad to come home after visiting her. My grandmother had told me that it was because she had no teeth left, but still, I didn't like the way her lips seemed to disappear into her mouth in a network of tiny wrinkles.

"You may find this hard to imagine," my grandmother said, "but Nehama was the most beautiful young girl in the whole city. Her skin was like cream, her hair like the finest silk, reaching almost to her waist. Matchmakers came from far and wide to try and arrange a marriage between Nehama and this or that or the other eligible young man. But this story is not about Nehama, but about her grandmother. She told it to Nehama's mother, Nehama's mother told it to her, she told it to me, and now I'm telling it to you. So listen.

Nehama's grandmother was called Ruth. Ruth was a beautiful young woman, but not only beautiful. She was kind-hearted and clever as well. A marriage had been arranged between her and a young man called Asher. On the day that they were introduced, they fell madly in love, and so, as you can imagine, everything was perfect. It was autumn. Ruth and her mother planned to spend the winter sewing and embroidering sheets, pillowcases, towels, tablecloths, and aprons, not to mention preparing drawers full of camisoles and dainty petticoats and delicate blouses. Then, in the spring, for the wedding Ruth would be dressed in a white lace dress with a veil over her face, ready to stand with her beloved Asher under the red velvet canopy which represented the groom's home, and into which he would welcome his bride.

Well, all that sewing and preparation could not possibly be

done by Ruth and her mother working by themselves, so all the ladies of the family helped. Ruth's friends came to lend their hands to the task as well, and winter evening after winter evening passed in this way; with skillful hands moving like butterflies over the fabric in the yellow light of lamps. In the corners of the room, over the shoulders of the women sewing, the shadows trembled and shook and stretched. Voices grew quiet and it was quite natural at such a time that minds turned to such things as the spirits of the dead. One particular story was told that saddened Ruth greatly, because she could put herself in the place of the bride in the story, and imagine . . . well, let me tell you the tale as her friends told it to Ruth.

Once, they said, there was a bride who died on the very day of her wedding. In fact she died as she was waiting to walk with her mother and the groom's mother to the bridal canopy. The groom came before the ceremony to look under her veil. This is a tradition that makes quite sure the bride is the one the man has agreed to marry. When this poor groom lifted the veil, there was his future wife pale and waxen as a lily, with all the life gone from her. The rejoicing for the wedding gave way to seven days of black mourning. Tears flowed like wine. But time passed, and gradually the young man grew more interested in life than in remembering his dead bride, and at last, another marriage was arranged for him. But the ghost of the first bride was still wandering the face of the earth, weeping her love. The long and the short of it was: the new bride called off the wedding twenty-four hours before the ceremony, claiming to have seen a specter dressed in bridal clothes standing at the foot of her bed.

'You should be careful, Ruth,' said all Ruth's friends. 'People say the ghost still visits weddings to this day. What would you do if you saw her? Would you faint?' Ruth answered not a word, but smiled over her stitching.

The days passed and the nights too, and soon the spring came, and it was time for Ruth and Asher to be married. The night before her wedding, when Ruth went into her bedroom to spend her last night under her father's roof, she saw the thin figure of a young girl dressed in white, sitting on the end of her bed and weeping. Ruth knew at once that this was the ghost her friends had spoken of, but so heart-rending was the sound of the ghost's tears, that Ruth was moved to pity.

'What's the matter?' she whispered. 'Why are you crying?'

'I am crying,' said the ghost, 'because there is to be a wedding and it is not my wedding.'

'But you wouldn't want it to be your wedding,' said Ruth, 'because the person I am marrying is not your love, but mine.'

The ghost turned a stricken face to Ruth. 'But I never stood under the canopy and saw it all twined around with flowers. I never heard the Seven Blessings. No one put a ring on my finger, and I have never heard the glass being crushed beneath my husband's foot. If only I could be part of the ceremony, I could rest easy in my grave forever.'

Ruth took a deep breath. 'Stay here,' she said, 'and I will speak to my mother.' She left the room. After an hour, she returned. The ghost was still sitting at the foot of the bed.

'I have spoken to my mother,' said Ruth. 'You may take her place tomorrow. Do you promise to go back to where you came from if I let you stand at my side throughout the ceremony?' The ghost nodded and vanished into thin air.

The next day, Ruth's mother and her friends helped her dress and prepare for the wedding. Lighted candles stood on the table, together with small cut-glass bowls of sugared almonds and raisins for the bride's attendants. Ruth, of course, was not allowed to eat anything until after the wedding.

When Asher came to raise the veil, he found the most beautiful bride in the whole world waiting for him, dressed in white lace like foam, her eyes shining like diamonds.

The guests started to whisper to themselves as the bridal procession made its way to the canopy. The marriage contract had been read, and all was ready for the ceremony.

'But where is the bride's mother?' people said. 'Who is that standing at Ruth's left hand?'

The Rabbi sang the Seven Blessings, the wine was drunk, and at last the glass, wrapped in a white cloth, was crushed under the groom's heel, to symbolize the destruction of the Temple in Jerusalem, and to remind everyone that even in the midst of joy, there were people suffering, somewhere in the world. And through everything, the ghost stood beside the bride, under a velvet canopy at last.

Later, as the music rose into the night sky, and everyone was dancing and making merry, the ghost tapped Ruth on the shoulder.

'Thank you,' she said. 'I will now rest easy in my grave, but I may return to dance at a wedding now and then, to remind myself of past happiness.'

She vanished then, and no one can be sure if she has ever returned. There is always someone, at every wedding party, someone at the edge of the dancing throng who may or may not be the ghost bride. No one asks any questions. They pour the guest another glass of wine, and move on, just in case . . . .

Ruth told Nehama's mother the story, and she told Nehama. I cannot vouch for the truth of it, of course, but I was at Nehama's wedding, and spoke for some minutes to a pale young woman whose name I didn't catch and whom I've never seen before or since."

My grandmother got up and went into the kitchen. I put the white shawl over my face like a veil, and looked through the tracery of flowers and leaves at my image in the glass, pretending to be the ghost-bride in my aunt Sara's high-heeled silver sandals.

Later on, my grandmother came to put the shawls away, and helped me to get ready for bed. First, I put on my nightdress, then she brought me a drink of warm milk with honey stirred into it. She waited while I brushed my teeth, and then sat on my bed for a few moments. During the winter months, I always had a fluffy dark blue blanket on my bed. It was exactly the color of the night sky and was bound around the edges with a wide blue satin ribbon that I stroked as I fell asleep.

My grandmother left the light on in the corridor. I watched her shadow disappearing and listened to the comforting sound of her voice, rising and falling in the room next to mine.

Property of

BRIDGEPORT PUBLIC LIBRARY

OLD MILL GREEN LIBRARY